Zak shot from the free throw line as A.J. leaped in vain. Zak was short, but he was quick and strong.

Swish! It was six up.

"If I play school league basketball, I'll miss student council meetings at noon. If I go to the meetings, I'll miss basketball this year." A.J. drove for the basket again.

Swish! Eight to six.

Zak's ball. "Miss basketball? Our power forward? I can't believe you'd even think of missing basketball!"

Be sure to read all the books in the Golden Rule Duo series:

And the Winner Is . . .
Trick 'N' Trouble
The Chosen Ones
Time Out!

Time Out!

by Janet Holm McHenry
Illustrated by Donna Kae Nelson

Chariot Books™
*A Division of Cook
Communications Ministries*

Chariot Books™ is an imprint of Chariot Family Publishing
Cook Communications Ministries, Elgin, Illinois 60120
Cook Communications Ministries, Paris, Ontario
Kingsway Communications, Eastbourne, England

TIME OUT!

Scripture quotations are from the Holy Bible, New International Version,
© 1973, 1978, 1984 by International Bible Society. Used by permission of
Zondervan Publishing House. All rights reserved.

Designed by Larry Taylor
First Printing, 1995
Printed in the United States of America
99 98 97 96 95 5 4 3 2 1

Library of Congress Cataloging-in-Publication Data
Available upon request.

Do to others
as you would have them
do to you.
Luke 6:31

Contents

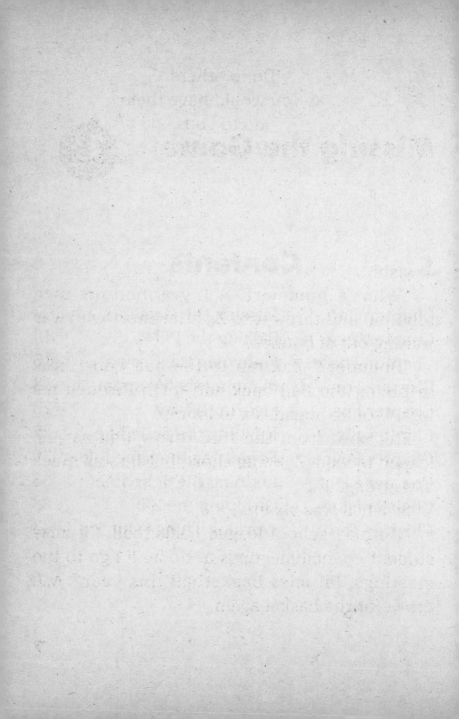

Missing the Game

Swish!

"What a bummer!" A.J. grabbed his own rebound and threw it to Zak the Short who was waiting out of bounds.

"Bummer?" Zak ran to the half court line, dribbling the ball back and forth through his legs. "You're ahead, six to four."

Zak shot from the free throw line as A.J. leaped in vain. Zak was short, but he was quick and strong.

Swish! It was six up.

"If I play school league basketball, I'll miss student council meetings at noon. If I go to the meetings, I'll miss basketball this year." A.J. drove for the basket again.

Swish! Eight to six.

Zak's ball. "Miss basketball? Our power forward? I can't believe you'd even think of missing basketball!"

"But you don't get it, Zak. I'd miss two meetings a week and have to quit student council. Don't you remember how hard we worked in September to get me elected?"

Zak stopped for a moment and stared at him. A.J. used the opportunity to grab the ball. But Zak recovered and grabbed the ball back at A.J.'s first dribble. A fake, turn, jump shot.

Swish! Eight up.

Briiiiiiinnnnnggg. Recess was over at Pine Tree Elementary. The boys headed to the lineup for Mrs. Todd's fourth-grade class.

Zak put his arm around his best buddy. "A tie again. So what's the big deal? You said yourself the meetings were boring. What did you talk about last week?"

"The mess kids make in the cafeteria. And

whether to sell teddy bear pencils and sports pens in the student store."

"Wow!" Zak teased. "I sure wish I was on student council. I really love teddy bear pencils. Do you think the student council could get Barbie notebooks, too?"

A.J. pushed Zak away. "It's just harder than that, Zak. Those guys who voted for me—they expect me to do a good job. I swore an oath."

Zak looked at him. "No! Not in school!"

"Zak, you know what I mean! It was a pledge thing all the student council members had to say when we were elected. We made a commitment to stick to the job—no matter what."

The line started moving toward class.

Zak shook his head. "Well, if you change your mind, sign-ups are at noon. See Mr. Sizemore on the courts."

A.J. shook his head. He had to agree. Miss basketball? Nothing should make a guy miss basketball.

Picking the Pal

Back in class, A.J. rolled his eyes. His twin sister Emily had her hand up again. She always had some question or other.

"Mrs. Todd! Mrs. Todd!"

"Yes, Emily." At the front of the class the teacher scrunched her nose to push up her brown-framed glasses. She was pouring glitter into cups while the last of the class got their drinks after recess.

"It's December, Mrs. Todd," Emily said, pointing to the wall. "You owe me five in Mouse Money."

"You're right. I forgot to change the calendar." Mrs. Todd reached into her pocket. "Here's your five for catching me in a mistake. The classroom fun store will be open on the last day of the month, Emily. You can do your shopping with it then. And speaking of shopping, before you know it, Christmas will be here."

Christmas. That was the wrong thing to say. The room exploded with chattering voices.

"Okay, okay," Mrs. Todd hushed the classroom. But when she waved her arms, she knocked over the pile of Styrofoam balls that had been stacked near the glitter.

A.J. shook his head. That was normal for Mrs. Todd.

"Before we start our comet project," she said, picking up the balls, "I want to remind you to remember your secret pal. Most of you picked a name at the beginning of December. Some people haven't heard anything yet, and it's been over a week since we started this."

A couple of heads nodded.

Zak raised his hand. "Mine gave me a pack of

baseball cards today."

"That's nice," Mrs. Todd said, "but you don't need to give a gift. Just write a nice note each day and leave it on the bookcase by the door."

Zak leaned over to A.J. "And how many ways can you say 'Merry Christmas'?"

Mrs. Todd looked at Zak. "You can say more than Merry Christmas. You can say something nice about a project they did or encourage them to do well on a test. You can write a poem or words to a favorite song. You don't need to give anything that costs money."

A.J. shook his head. Last month it was acorn mush for Thanksgiving. This month it was secret pals for Christmas. Nothing was ordinary with Mrs. Todd.

Even worse, A.J. hadn't heard a thing from his secret pal. He'd been pretty good about remembering his—Tyler. He had given him a stick of gum one day and some Mouse Money another day. A.J. had even given Tyler his

"Good for One Homework Assignment Coupon" that he had won when he got a hundred percent on his spelling test last week. And that was pretty amazing, since he was flunking spelling in October.

A.J. looked around the room, trying to figure out who had his name. Several girls smiled at him. He hoped it wasn't a girl. Girls did weird stuff. He almost liked it better in third grade when the girls just left him alone. But this year it was different. They were bugging him all the time.

But girls were pretty good about things like secret pals. It probably wasn't a girl. Maybe it was somebody who had been absent. Jeff was still absent with the chicken pox. Maybe it was Jeff.

Mrs. Todd started passing out the Styrofoam balls to the desk groups. That was the wrong thing to do. When she turned back for the yarn and glitter, balls floated from one end of the room to the other. Boys quickly made a

basketball game by holding out their baseball hats. Almost anything could become a basketball game that time of year.

A.J. caught another Styrofoam ball in his hat. *God, you know how much I love basketball. Should I quit student council, God?*

I'll ask the guys at lunchtime. Maybe they'll have some ideas.

14

Following the Crowd

Will you quit bugging me?"

As A.J. was leaving the cafeteria at lunchtime, Emily cornered him at the door.

"But I've got this great idea!" she said. "Look!"

Emily had a small piece of paper. On it was written:

G.L.O.W.

"Glow? So?" A.J. looked around to make sure his friends weren't watching.

"G-L-O-W. God's Light of the World. I want to start a Bible study here at school called GLOW."

"So? Start a Bible study. It's a free world, Emmo. Do what you want."

CHAPTER THREE

Emily sighed. "I thought you might like to help start it—you know, invite your friends like Zak and Mike and Tyler."

"I don't think so, Emmo. They teased me forever when I talked about God stuff a couple of months ago. They'd never go to a Bible study."

"How do you know unless you ask? Some Christian you are, A.J."

A.J. shuffled his feet. "Well, whatever, Emmo. Here are the guys. I've gotta go. I'll see ya."

"Come on, A.J.!" Zak was waving.

"Yeah, come on!" said Mike.

"We're late for basketball sign-ups!" said Tyler.

A.J. hurried off with his three friends to the playground where Mr. Sizemore, the tall, thin fifth-grade teacher, was standing with a clipboard. In front of him across the two basketball courts was a long line of boys and girls shivering. There wasn't snow yet in

Mountain Valley, but even if there were, that wouldn't stop the Pine Tree kids from playing basketball.

A.J. slowed when he saw the long line.

Zak turned. "Hey, what's the deal, A.J.?"

"Just go sign me up. I've got a student council meeting. I'm already late."

Zak's eyes popped open. "You're going to student council on a day like this?"

"I don't have a choice, Zak. I'm stuck going to a boring student council meeting."

"A.J., you do have a choice. Basketball is the coolest time of year. You and I—we're a team."

"Well, I hope so," said A.J. "But today— please just sign me up."

A.J. turned toward the office on the lowest level of the four-tiered school that was built into the mountainside. He hesitated again, looking at the lineup of kids.

I hope we talk about more than just teddy bear pencils.

Planning the Program

Rats! The only empty chair in the meeting room was right next to Mr. Lightfoot. There was no way A.J. could slip in without being seen.

The big, strong principal was standing at the other end of the room in front of a white erasable board. He had a blue marker in his hand. He gave A.J. a stern look as A.J. sat down.

"All right, the decorations committee has everything arranged for the Christmas program. Good job, girls."

Mr. Lightfoot flipped through his spiral notebook. Mr. Lightfoot wrote everything in his spiral notebook.

A.J. looked around the long table. The class

presidents and representatives were all there. And of those twelve, there was only one other boy on the council—Carlos Sanchez, the fourth-grade president, who was next to A.J.

A.J. shook his head. That meant a whole mob of girls at the meetings. Most of them giggled when he was around. He knew they liked him, and that was sort of okay, but he just wasn't ready for girls yet.

He looked sideways and noticed for the first time that Emily was sitting with the girls at the other end of the table. *Emily? She's not on student council. Why is she here?*

He rolled his eyes again. Emily had her hand up. She always had her hand up.

"Mr. Lightfoot, Mr. Lightfoot!" she said.

Mr. Lightfoot crossed something out in his notebook. "Yes, Emily. Welcome to our meeting. Do you have a request for the student council?"

"Yes. I heard student council is organizing the school Christmas program and I have a

request for this year."

"Certainly—go ahead."

"Well, some of us girls," she emphasized, looking pointedly at A.J., "are organizing a Bible study at Pine Tree."

Mr. Lightfoot raised his eyebrows. "Yes?"

"And we think it would be great if we had real Christmas music at the Christmas program."

20

"Real Christmas music? I thought we did have real Christmas music."

A.J. pulled his baseball hat down and slumped a little in his chair.

"No, we don't," she said. "Oh, we do 'Jingle Bells' and 'Rudolph the Red-Nosed Reindeer,' but we don't do any real Christmas carols—like 'Silent Night' or 'O Come, All Ye Faithful.' You know, ones about Jesus."

Mr. Lightfoot cleared his throat. "Well, I don't know. We've always done the other kind. It's up to the teachers to decide what they want to do. So you might ask your teacher—Mrs. Todd?—or the others."

He cleared his throat again, adjusting his tie. "Thank you, Emily. Now, where were we? Oh, yes, the program schedule."

He turned toward A.J. who was sitting right next to him, "And A.J., how is the schedule coming along?"

A.J. turned pale and his mouth dropped a

little. "Ummm, schedule? Oh, ummm, just fine."

Mr. Lightfoot turned toward the board again. "So then, do you have the information from the teachers about what each class will do?"

A.J. cleared his throat. "It's, ummm, ah . . . "

Mr. Lightfoot crossed his arms, turning around. "A.J., did you make the sign-up sheet for the Christmas program and find out what each teacher plans to do?"

"No, I forgot, Mr. Lightfoot."

Mr. Lightfoot breathed in deeply and blew out through his mouth. "Anthony, I need the information in two days so we can get the programs typed and printed. Do you understand?"

A.J. nodded. "You want the sign-up by Friday?"

"Right. Meet with me in my office Friday at noon. I'm counting on you, A.J."

"Okay, Mr. Lightfoot. I won't let you down."

Figuring a Way

A.J. hurried out of the office building and looked down the school hill. "Zak! Hey, Zak!"

Zak and buddies were practicing free throws. A.J. took the twenty-one steps down to the playground two at a time. Zak tossed him the ball as he approached the court, and A.J. dribbled the ball to the group.

"Did you sign me up?"

"Yeah, it's going to be great. You and I, we're both on the Cougars. There are four teams of fourth graders, and there are just six guys on each team. We'll all get a lot of playing time with just one sub."

A.J. scratched his head as Zak listed the

other players' names. Practice would be on Tuesday and Thursday, games on Wednesday and Friday. The time clock would be shorter. . . .

But A.J.'s brain was in another court. A sub! Maybe he could sub in and out of games and still show up for student council meetings. He'd need some pretty fast feet, but maybe it would work!

"Zak, listen!"

"You listen, Anthony Jacob!" It was Emily. Behind her were two other girls.

"Some other time, Emmo." A.J. turned toward the hoop and took a shot.

Emily followed him as he went to the end of the free throw line. "No, now, Dummo. Why didn't you speak up at the student council meeting about the Christmas carols? I thought you'd take my side."

"There aren't sides yet, Emmo. You heard Mr. Lightfoot. He said to talk to the teachers."

"Well, you're in charge of the Christmas

sign-ups. You could at least have said it was a good idea. You know what Dad said last night."

"About Christian things at school?"

"Yeah. He said we could have our Bible study, if we girls organize it ourselves."

A.J. nodded. "I know. And he said we could have carols about Jesus as long as they're old ones—what's that word?"

"Traditional. And Dad should know—he's a history teacher and knows that kind of stuff."

Zak passed the ball to A.J. who was back at the front of the line. A.J. dribbled in place for a moment or two and then stopped, holding the ball under his right arm. "Can you just take your Bible study group and go somewhere else, Emmo? I'm kind of busy right now."

He turned, jumped, and shot. The ball completely missed the rim, just brushing the bottom of the net. "Air ball!" yelled the others behind him, laughing and pointing at A.J.

A.J. gave Emily a dirty look and ignored her as she walked away.

The bell rang and students lined up for class.

Zak joined A.J. at the end of the line, fingering the ball. "Hey, A.J., cool ball, huh? Got it from my secret pal. It's been used a little, but it's still neat."

"Yeah, you're lucky, Zak. I haven't gotten anything yet."

"Hey, I'd be mad."

"Yeah, if I don't get something soon . . ."

"Maybe it's Emily, A.J., and she's getting you back for not joining her little Bible group. I heard they're the glow worms or something. Gonna be a little glow worm, A.J.?"

A.J. gave Zak a dirty look and otherwise tried to ignore him.

God, why did You have to make my twin sister a girl?

Hustling the Schedule

On Thursday A.J. was busy. From one teacher to another he hurried—before school, at recess. And at lunch he tried it—subbing in and out of the practice game. He used every excuse in the book and more so he could catch teachers as they were coming and going.

By the time his bus came at the end of the day, A.J. had almost all of the teachers signed up for the Christmas program.

Almost all. There was only one problem. Mrs. Todd was absent that day, so his list was not complete. *I'll catch her tomorrow,* A.J. thought as he folded the piece of paper and put it in his pants pocket.

CHAPTER SIX

"A.J.!"

A.J. turned as he was about to step into his bus. Towering over him was Mr. Sizemore.

"A.J., don't pull that one again."

"What's that, Mr. Sizemore?"

"The disappearing act. You need to stick with your team all the way, even in just a practice. Tomorrow is your first real game against the Colts."

"Yes, sir! I'll be there. You can count on me."

A.J. hopped onto the bus and squeezed down the aisle. At the back Zak was waving. "Hey, man, you about missed the bus."

A.J. sat down next to Zak. "I had to get all the teachers to sign up on this schedule thing. What did you think of basketball?"

"Fine, if you'd stuck around the whole time. With these twenty-minute games, we're going to need you every second, A.J. Our team is going to be the pits unless you're there. Only you and I can shoot. Don't let us down, A.J."

The bus slowed to a stop and Zak got up. "See you at noon, 'pardner,' " he said, shooting from the hip.

That Zak—he was weird at times. But noon. What was at noon? *Oh, rats! The meeting with Mr. Lightfoot is at noon. Well, I'll give the schedule to Mr. L. and then run to my game. He just wants the list. It'll work out. I think.*

Forgetting the Schedule

A.J. had a sinking feeling when he stepped off the bus the next morning.

"Hey, Dummo." It was Emily. "Come to our Bible study today? We're going to meet in Mrs. Todd's room every Friday right after school. So far there's three of us. Me, Maria, and the new girl, Rachel. She seems kind of interested."

"Nah, not today. I've got something to do. If I could just remember . . . " He started walking toward the courts where several boys were shooting baskets.

"Oh, did you remember that paper airplane you made last night for your secret pal?" asked Emily.

"Yeah, got it right here. I wrote all the spelling words on it so Tyler can practice them."

"I think this secret pal thing is neat. I got a cute bookmark yesterday. Oh, did you see what Bo got yesterday? He got a Snickers bar! He says he's been getting all kinds of stuff— sometimes two things in a day."

A.J. sputtered. "Oh, that's great. I haven't gotten a thing yet. Now how fair is that when I put something out every day and I don't get anything back? Somebody like that shouldn't even pick a secret pal if they don't plan to do it."

"Maybe it's somebody who's been absent, like Jeff."

"Mmmmm . . ." Absent. That reminded A.J. of something. . . . *Oh, I've got to get Mrs. Todd's Christmas program plan before school. Whew! Good thing I remembered.*

A.J. reached into his pocket. He had put the

schedule there. Not in the left pocket. Not in the right pocket. Not in the back pocket.

Oh, no, those were yesterday's pants. *What am I going to do God?*

Emily was giving him the eye. He couldn't let on. She'd tell someone.

"See you, Em. I've got to take care of something."

Redoing the Schedule

"Zak! Zak!" A.J. ran to where Zak was playing hoops with the guys.

"Yeah, A.J., what?" Zak rested his hands on his knees to catch his breath in the cold morning air.

"I need your help with something fast. I've got to get the teachers to sign up on the Christmas program schedule."

"Didn't you do that yesterday?"

"Yeah, I did, but I left it at home. And if Mr. Lightfoot doesn't get it this noon, I'm going to be dead meat."

"Call home and ask your mom to bring it."

A.J. looked at his friend. "You mean, ask Mrs. Noway to use the phone?"

Zak shook his head in fear.

Zak must not have been thinking. Mrs. Noway was the office clerk. That wasn't really her name. It was Mrs. Norway. But all the kids called her Mrs. Noway, because that was what she said when a kid asked to use the phone: "No way! Are you bleeding? Is a bone broken? Did you throw up? If not, no way and out the door!"

"Come on, Zak!" A.J. said.

Zak looked back at the guys who were yelling at him to join the game again. "Okay, just let me finish this game."

A.J. pulled on his arm. "Zak, I need your help now. You check in the classrooms. I'll go to the office. Just tell the teachers that I lost the other schedule. Here's a piece of paper and a pencil to write it down."

"Okay, A.J. But you owe me one, buddy."

A.J. watched Zak run up the eighty-four steps to the top level of classrooms. A.J. headed for the first level.

Let's see. About half of the teachers will be in their rooms getting things ready for the day. The other half will be in the teachers' room next to the office. Drinking coffee, A.J. thought. *Mom said it was only about fifteen degrees this morning.*

A.J. pulled open the office door and stepped in quietly. To get to the teachers' room, he had to sneak by Mrs. Noway. He was in luck. She was filing, with her back turned. He started to tiptoe to the right toward the teachers' room door, but just as he was about to round the corner, the file drawer clicked shut and Mrs. Noway turned around.

"Yes, young man! Oh, it's you, A.J."

"Yes, Mrs. No . . . I mean, yes, ma'am. I just need to get the teachers to sign this form for the Christmas program. It's something Mr. Lightfoot needs at noon today."

Mrs. Noway took the paper from his hand. "There's nothing on this, A.J."

"Well, I know, ma'am, but there will be when I talk to them. I just need a couple minutes."

She took her reading glasses off and peered at A.J. He tried to look at her but found his eyes wandering about everywhere else. Then Mrs. Todd came out of the teachers' room.

Mrs. Todd! Relief! She was carrying loosely rolled butcher paper about the size of a sleeping bag. "Oh, A.J., help me with this, please!" At that moment the whole mess slipped through her arms and rolled to her feet.

A.J. put his paper and pencil in his pocket and kneeled down to scoop up the paper. He blurted his problem to Mrs. Todd, and she agreed to get the program plans from the teachers in the teachers' room if he'd carry the paper to her room.

Great, thought A.J. *I can see how Zak is doing getting the others.* But as he started up the next set of stairs, he met Zak coming down them.

"Wow!" said A.J. "Are you done already?"

Zak handed him the paper. "Hey, sorry, buddy. I couldn't find anyone. The door was locked."

A.J. gave Zak a dirty look. "Sure, buddy, and with the whole minute you took, you really tried. Thanks for nothing."

A.J. stared at the crumpled piece of paper in his hand. Now what would he do?

Dropping the Ball

A.J. looked at his watch. It was 8:15, fifteen minutes until school started. He headed up to the top level of classrooms, but he couldn't go as quickly as he wanted because there was ice on the stairs from the morning's dew.

He was just a few steps from the top when he saw Mr. Sizemore dash out the doors with a large box in his hands. If A.J. hurried, he could catch the door before it locked shut. He took the last two steps in one leap, but Mr. Sizemore hadn't seen him coming and . . .

BAM! All in an instant, Mr. Sizemore hit the ice, knocking A.J. off his feet. Mr. Sizemore slid on the top step and lost his footing too. Both tried

to steady the other, but it was too slick.

A.J. landed on his seat and skidded down a few steps. Mr. Sizemore landed on his seat with the box upside down on his head. Dozens of plastic metric cups and beakers bounced down the hillside. And the very long roll of butcher paper A.J. had been carrying for Mrs. Todd rolled down to the third level.

"Sorry," they said at the same instant.

"Oh, boy!" said Mr. Sizemore, looking down the steps. "Mrs. Moore needs to use these metric things first thing this morning."

A.J. looked down the steps. The cups and beakers were scattered down the hill. He knew he should help Mr. Sizemore pick them up, but if he did, he wouldn't get to all the teachers. A.J. quickly started to roll up the butcher paper.

He finished rolling up the paper and started for the door. But something made him turn around. Mr. Sizemore was inching down the slippery stairs, dragging the box, which bumped from step to step. With each step he picked up one or two containers and put them in the box.

Gee, what a mess, thought A.J. *He'll never get all this picked up before the kids come running up here. But I don't have time. . . .*

He tried the door. It was open! Mr. Sizemore must have unlocked it or . . . maybe Zak never tried to open it at all. Some friend!

Just like my secret pal. . . . Some pal. He's let me down too.

What's that verse Emily's always saying, God? Do to others as you would have them do to you? Luke, ummmm, 6:31? People sure aren't doing to me as I'd like.

Mrs. Todd's room was locked. A.J. looked around. None of the other classroom doors was open. He set the crumpled butcher paper in front of her door.

A.J. checked his watch. Only ten minutes left until the bell rang. And he still needed to check the five classrooms on this level and the others on levels two and three.

He hesitated, looking out the doors at Mr. Sizemore inching down the stairs.

God, I haven't been a very good Christian. I let down Mr. Lightfoot. I've been Dummo Brother. And now I've left Mr. Sizemore with a mess.

God, I messed up the other things, but I can help Mr. Sizemore now. I guess I'll just take the heat for the rest as it comes.

A.J. ran out the doors, down to Mr. Sizemore.

"A.J. You're back."

"Yeah, I had to do something for Mr. L., but I figured you need my help more."

Mr. Sizemore rubbed his back. "Thanks, A.J., but what are you doing for Mr. Lightfoot?"

"I'm supposed to find out what the teachers are going to do for the Christmas program."

"Didn't you do that yesterday?"

A.J. nodded. "It's a long story."

"You're on student council, aren't you?"

"Yeah—until noon today, anyway." A.J. picked up several more cups and put them in the box.

"A.J., how are you playing basketball when you have student council meetings, too?"

A.J. gulped. He'd been found out. "Umm, that's kind of a big problem, Mr. Sizemore. They're both at the same time some days."

Mr. Sizemore nodded. "Well, A.J., let me see what I can do."

Working Things Out

A.J. ran to the end of the line. Zak filed in behind him. "Hey, A.J., did you see all the teachers?"

"Nope."

"So you don't have the sign-up ready?"

"Nope."

The line began to move.

"So you're not going to be able to play ball?"

"Nope."

"No power forward for the Cougars again. Guess it's up to Zak the Short to save the day."

A.J. moaned.

"Hey, look what I've got for Bo today," said Zak. He was holding a Lakers key chain.

"Hey, wait a minute!" cried Mike, who was

ahead of them in line. "Bo is my secret pal."

"No he's not," said Zak. "See—I still have his name." He reached into his coat pocket and pulled out a small piece of paper neatly folded four times. On it was a messy cursive:

A.J. squinted at it. It looked familiar. He took the paper from Zak and turned it over. "Zak, you nutso, this is my name—see?"

Sure enough, upside down it read:

"You were supposed to be giving to ME all this time. No wonder I didn't get anything from my secret pal. I don't know about you, Isaac!"

The boys filed into the classroom, took off their coats, and sat at their desks. Most of the class studied for the spelling test. Tyler sailed his secret pal paper airplane. Mike tried to make a replica. And Emily gave A.J. The Look.

Maybe I'll try Emily's Bible study, thought A.J. *Just once, at least. But GLOW has gotta go.*

As Mrs. Todd was about to give the spelling test, Mr. Lightfoot walked in. He talked to Mrs. Todd for a minute. She nodded, pointed, and Mr. Lightfoot walked over to A.J.

Oh, no, Mr. Sizemore told Mr. Lightfoot about me knocking him over. Or worse, he knows about the Christmas program sign-ups.

A.J. slumped into his chair, trying to disappear.

"A.J., I'd like to speak with you, please."

A.J. looked up and grinned weakly. They walked over to the classroom door.

"Mr. Lightfoot, I can explain. Knocking over Mr. Sizemore—that was an accident. And about the Christmas program . . . well . . ."

Mr. Lightfoot cleared his throat. "A.J., I heard about the accident. Mr. Sizemore said you were quite the gentleman to help him pick things up when you needed to do something yourself."

"Well, uh, I was trying to get to all the

teachers about the program."

"That's what I figured. Do you have the schedule now?"

"I had it all done yesterday, but I left it at home. Mrs. Todd got some of the teachers to do it again today, but I . . . " A.J. hung his head. "No, it's not done."

"A.J., because you helped someone, I'm going to help you. Can you get the sign-up done right now if Mrs. Todd excuses you from the spelling test? She just told me she would.

"You can bring the schedule to me when you get it done. Then you won't have to miss your game. We'll work our student council meetings around the basketball schedule. That's only fair to all the students who want to do both."

A.J.'s mouth dropped open and his eyes nearly popped out as he watched Mr. Lightfoot leave. His eyes must have still looked buggy when he walked to Mrs. Todd's desk.

"Are you all right, A.J.?" she asked.

"I think so," said A.J. "It's just that one minute my life is a mess and the next it's great. And I didn't do a thing. It just happened—like night turning into day."

Mrs. Todd smiled. "Oh, I think you had something to do with it. And speaking of night, you'll want to get back to class quickly."

"Yeah?"

"We're going to practice our song for the Christmas program—'Silent Night.'"

A.J. smiled as he walked back to his seat to get the sign-up sheet. He knew Emily would be happy they were going to sing a "real" Christmas carol. Actually, he was too. He was kind of tired of singing "Jingle bells, shotgun shells."

That was third grade stuff. He was in the fourth grade now. Things were different. He could almost dribble the ball between his legs. And people looked up to him. Even girls.

Oh, brother, those girls are looking at me again. I hate it when they do that. I'd rather take a spelling test than have girls stare at me.

Then it dawned on him. A.J. raised his hand.

"Yes, A.J.?"

"I'll just run that errand now, Mrs. Todd."

Mrs. Todd nodded and waved.

The way A.J. figured it, he could get out of a spelling test and get away from the girls at the same time. Now, who could beat that?